HORRID HENRY
AND THE
MEGA–MEAN
TIME MACHINE

Francesca Simon
Illustrated by Tony Ross

Orion
Children's Books

For my sister, Anne Simon,
who reminded me about
our time machine

First published in Great Britain in 2005
by Orion Children's Books
Reissued in paperback 2008
by Orion Children's Books
a division of the Orion Publishing Group Ltd
Orion House
5 Upper Saint Martin's Lane
London WC2H 9EA
An Hachette UK Company

The Orion Publishing Group's policy is to use papers that are natural,
renewable and recyclable products and made from wood grown in
sustainable forests. The logging and manufacturing processes are expected to
conform to the environmental regulations of the country of origin.

A catalogue record for this book is available from the British Library.

Printed in Great Britain by Clays Ltd, St Ives plc

www.horridhenry.co.uk
www.orionbooks.co.uk

HORRID HENRY
AND THE
MEGA–MEAN
TIME MACHINE

Francesca Simon spent her childhood on the beach in California, and then went to Yale and Oxford Universities to study medieval history and literature. She now lives in London with her family. She has written over 45 books and won the Children's Book of the Year in 2008 at the Galaxy British Book Awards for *Horrid Henry and the Abominable Snowman*.

Also by Francesca Simon

Don't Cook Cinderella
Helping Hercules

and for younger readers
Don't Be Horrid, Henry

The Topsy-Turvies
Illustrated by Emily Bolam

There is a complete list of **Horrid Henry** titles
at the end of the book.
Horrid Henry is also available on audio CD and
digital download, all read by Miranda Richardson.

Visit Horrid Henry's website at
www.horridhenry.co.uk for competitions,
games, downloads and a monthly newsletter

CONTENTS

1

HORRID HENRY'S HIKE

Horrid Henry looked out of the window. AAARRRGGGHHH! It was a lovely day. The sun was shining. The birds were tweeting. The breeze was blowing. Little fluffy clouds floated by in a bright blue sky.

Rats.

Why couldn't it be raining? Or hailing? Or sleeting?

Any minute, any second, it would happen…the words he'd been dreading, the words he'd give anything not to hear, the words –

'Henry! Peter! Time to go for a walk,' called Mum.

'Yippee!' said Perfect Peter. 'I can wear my new yellow wellies!'

'NO!' screamed Horrid Henry.

Go for a walk! Go for a walk! Didn't he walk enough already? He walked to school. He walked home from school. He walked to the TV. He walked to the computer. He walked to the sweet jar *and* all the way back to the comfy black chair.

Horrid Henry walked plenty. Ugghh. The last thing he needed was more walking. More chocolate, yes. More crisps, yes. More *walking*? No way! Why oh why couldn't his parents ever say, 'Henry! Time to play on the computer.' Or 'Henry, stop doing your homework this minute! Time to turn on the TV.'

But no. For some reason his mean, horrible parents thought he spent too much time sitting indoors. They'd been threatening for weeks to make him go on a family walk. Now the dreadful moment had come. His precious weekend was ruined.

Horrid Henry hated nature. Horrid Henry hated fresh air. What could be more boring than walking up and down streets staring at lamp posts? Or sloshing across some stupid muddy park? Nature smelled. Uggh! He'd much rather be inside watching TV.

Mum stomped into the sitting room. 'Henry! Didn't you hear me calling?'

'No,' lied Henry.

'Get your wellies on, we're going,' said

3

Dad, rubbing his hands. 'What a lovely day.'

'I don't want to go for a walk,' said Henry. 'I want to watch *Rapper Zapper Zaps Terminator Gladiator.*'

'But Henry,' said Perfect Peter, 'fresh air and exercise are so good for you.'

'I don't care!' shrieked Henry.

Horrid Henry stomped downstairs and flung open the front door. He breathed in deeply, hopped on one foot, then shut the door.

'There! Done it. Fresh air *and* exercise,' snarled Henry.

'Henry, we're going,' said Mum. 'Get in the car.'

Henry's ears pricked up.

'The car?' said Henry. 'I thought we were going for a walk.'

'We are,' said Mum. 'In the countryside.'

'Hurray!' said Perfect Peter. 'A nice *long* walk.'

'NOOOO!' howled Henry. Plodding along in the boring old park was bad enough, with its mouldy leaves and dog poo and stumpy trees. But at least the park wasn't very big. But the *countryside*?

The countryside was enormous! They'd be walking for hours, days, weeks, months, till his legs wore down to stumps and his feet fell off. And the countryside was so dangerous! Horrid Henry was sure he'd be swallowed up by quicksand or trampled to death by marauding chickens.

'I live in the city!' shrieked Henry. 'I don't want to go to the country!'

'Time you got out more,' said Dad.

'But look at those clouds,' moaned Henry, pointing to a fluffy wisp. 'We'll get soaked.'

'A little water never hurt anyone,' said Mum.

Oh yeah? Wouldn't they be sorry when he died of pneumonia.

'I'm staying here and that's final!' screamed Henry.

'Henry, we're waiting,' said Mum.

'Good,' said Henry.

'*I'm* all ready, Mum,' said Peter.

'I'm going to start deducting pocket money,' said Dad. '5p, 10p, 15p, 20 – '

Horrid Henry pulled on his wellies, stomped out of the door and got in the car. He slammed the door as hard as he could. It was so unfair! Why did he never get to do what *he* wanted to do? Now he would miss the first time Rapper Zapper had ever slugged it out with Terminator

Gladiator. And all because he had to go on a long, boring, exhausting, horrible hike. He was so miserable he didn't even have the energy to kick Peter.

'Can't we just walk round the block?' moaned Henry.

'N–O spells no,' said Dad. 'We're going for a lovely walk in the countryside and that's that.'

Horrid Henry slumped miserably in his seat. Boy would they be sorry when he was gobbled up by goats. Boo hoo, if only we hadn't gone on that walk in the wilds, Mum would wail.

Henry was right, we should have listened to him, Dad would sob. I miss Henry, Peter would howl. I'll never eat goat's cheese again. And now it's too late, they would shriek.

If only, thought Horrid Henry. That would serve them right.

All too soon, Mum pulled into a carpark, on the edge of a small wood.

'Wow,' said Perfect Peter. 'Look at all those lovely trees.'

'Bet there are werewolves hiding there,' muttered Henry.

'And I hope they come and eat *you*!'

'Mum!' squealed Peter. 'Henry's trying to scare me.'

'Don't be horrid, Henry,' said Mum.

Horrid Henry looked around him. There was a gate, leading to endless meadows bordered by hedgerows. A muddy path wound through the trees and across the fields. A church spire stuck up in the distance.

'Right, I've seen the countryside, let's go home,' said Henry.

Mum glared at him.

'What?' said Henry, scowling.

'Let's enjoy this lovely day,' said Dad, sighing.

'So what do we do now?' said Henry.

'Walk,' said Dad.

'Where?' said Henry.

'Just walk,' said Mum, 'and enjoy the beautiful scenery.'

Henry groaned.

9

'We're heading for the lake,' said Dad, striding off. 'I've brought bread and we can feed the ducks.'

'But *Rapper Zapper* starts in an hour!'

'Tough,' said Mum.

Mum, Dad, and Peter headed through the gate into the field. Horrid Henry trailed behind them walking as slowly as he could.

'Ahh, breathe the lovely fresh air,' said Mum.

'We should do this more often,' said Dad.

Henry sniffed.

The horrible smell of manure filled his nostrils.

10

'Ewww, smelly,' said Henry. 'Peter, couldn't you wait?'

'MUM!' shrieked Peter. 'Henry called me smelly.'

'Did not!'

'Did too!'

'Did not, smelly.'

'WAAAAAAAAA!' wailed Peter. 'Tell him to stop!'

'Don't be horrid, Henry!' screamed Mum. Her voice echoed. A dog walker passed her, and glared.

'Peter, would you rather run a mile, jump a stile, or eat a country pancake?' said Henry sweetly.

'Ooh,' said Peter. 'I love pancakes. And a

11

country one must be even more delicious than a city one.'

'Ha ha,' cackled Horrid Henry, sticking out his tongue. 'Fooled you. Peter wants to eat cowpats!'

'MUM!' screamed Peter.

Henry walked.

And walked.

And walked.

His legs felt heavier, and heavier, and heavier.

'This field is muddy,' moaned Henry.

'I'm bored,' groaned Henry.

'My feet hurt,' whined Henry.

'Can't we go home? We've already walked miles,' whinged Henry.

'We've been walking for ten minutes,' said Dad.

'Please can we go on walks more often,' said Perfect Peter. 'Oh, look at those fluffy little sheepies!'

Horrid Henry pounced. He was a zombie biting the head off the hapless human.

'AAAAEEEEEE!' squealed Peter.

'Henry!' screamed Mum.

'Stop it!' screamed Dad. 'Or no TV for a week.'

When he was king, thought Horrid Henry, any parent who made their children go on a hike would be dumped barefoot in a scorpion-infested desert.

Plod.

Plod.

Plod.

Horrid Henry dragged his feet. Maybe his horrible mean parents would get fed up waiting for him and turn back, he

13

thought, kicking some mouldy leaves.

Squelch.

Squelch.

Squelch.

Oh no, not *another* muddy meadow.

And then suddenly Horrid Henry had an idea. What was he thinking? All that fresh air must be rotting his brain. The sooner they got to the stupid lake, the sooner they could get home for the *Rapper Zapper Zaps Terminator Gladiator*.

'Come on, everyone, let's run!' shrieked Henry. 'Race you down the hill to the lake!'

'That's the spirit, Henry,' said Dad.

Horrid Henry dashed past Dad.

'OW!' shrieked Dad, tumbling into the stinging nettles.

Horrid Henry
whizzed past Mum.

'Eww!'
shrieked
Mum,
slipping
in a cowpat.

Splat!

Horrid Henry pushed past Peter.

'Waaa!' wailed Peter. 'My wellies are getting dirty.'

Horrid Henry scampered down the muddy path.

15

'Wait Henry!' yelped Mum. 'It's too slipp – aaaiiieeeee!'

Mum slid down the path on her bottom.

'Slow down!' puffed Dad.

'I can't run that fast,' wailed Peter.

But Horrid Henry raced on.

'Shortcut across the field!' he called. 'Come on slowcoaches!' The black and white cow grazing alone in the middle raised its head.

'Henry!' shouted Dad.

Horrid Henry kept running.

'I don't think that's a cow!' shouted Mum.

The cow lowered its head and charged.

'It's a bull!'

yelped Mum and Dad. 'RUN!'

'I said it was dangerous in the country-side!' gasped Henry, as everyone clambered over the stile in the nick of time. 'Look, there's the lake!' he added, pointing.

Henry ran down to the water's edge. Peter followed. The embankment narrowed to a point. Peter slipped past Henry and bagged the best spot, right at the water's edge where the ducks gathered.

'Hey, get away from there,' said Henry.

'I want to feed the ducks,' said Peter.

'*I* want to feed the ducks,' said Henry. 'Now move.'

'I was here first,' said Peter.

'Not any more,' said Henry.

Horrid Henry pushed Peter.

'Out of my way, worm!'

Perfect Peter pushed him back.

'Don't call me worm!'

Henry wobbled.

Peter wobbled.

Splash!

Peter tumbled into the lake.

Crash!

Henry tumbled into the lake.

'My babies!' shrieked Mum, jumping in after them.

'My – glug glug glug!' shrieked Dad, jumping into the muddy water after her.

'My new wellies!' gurgled Perfect Peter.

Bang!

Pow!

Terminator Gladiator slashed at Rapper Zapper.

Zap!

Rapper Zapper slashed back.

'Go Zappy!' yelled Henry, lying bundled up in blankets on the sofa. Once everyone had scrambled out of the lake, Mum and Dad had been keen to get home as fast as possible.

'I think the park next time,' mumbled Dad, sneezing.

'Definitely,' mumbled Mum, coughing.

'Oh, I don't know,' said Horrid Henry happily. 'A little water never hurt anyone.'

HORRID HENRY and THE MEGA-MEAN TIME MACHINE

Horrid Henry flicked the switch. The time machine whirred. Dials spun. Buttons pulsed. Latches locked. Horrid Henry Time Traveller was ready for blast off!

Now, where to go, where to go?

Dinosaurs, thought Henry. Yes! Henry loved dinosaurs. He would love to stalk a few Tyrannosaurus Rexes as they rampaged through the primordial jungle.

But what about King Arthur and the Knights of the Round Table? 'Arise, Sir Henry,' King Arthur would say, booting Lancelot out of his chair. 'Sure thing, King,' Sir Henry would reply, twirling his sword. 'Out of my way, worms!'

Or what about the siege of Troy?
Heroic Henry, that's who he'd be, the
fearless fighter dashing about doing daring
deeds.

Tempting, thought Henry. Very tempting.

Wait a sec, what about visiting the
future, where school was banned and
parents had to do whatever their children
told them? Where everyone had their
own spaceship and ate sweets for dinner.
And where King Henry the Horrible
ruled supreme, chopping off the head
of anyone who dared to say no to him.

To the future, thought Henry, setting
the dial.

Bang! Pow!

Henry braced himself for the jolt into
hyperspace – 10, 9, 8, 7, 6 –

'Henry, it's my turn.'

Horrid Henry ignored the alien's whine.

– 5, 4, 3 –

'Henry! If you don't share I'm going to tell Mum.'

AAAARRRRGGGHHHHHH. The Time Machine juddered to a halt. Henry climbed out.

'Go away, Peter,' said Henry. 'You're spoiling everything.'

'But it's my turn.'

'GO AWAY!'

'Mum said we could *both* play with the

box,' said Peter. 'We could cut out windows, make a little house, paint flowers – '

'NO!' screeched Henry.

'But...' said Peter. He stood in the sitting room, holding his scissors and crayons.

'Don't you touch my box!' hissed Henry.

'I will if I want to,' said Peter. 'And it's not yours.' Henry had no right to boss him around, thought Peter. He'd been waiting such a long time for his turn. Well, he wasn't waiting any longer. He'd start cutting out a window this minute.

Peter got out his scissors.

'Stop! It's a time machine, you toad!' shrieked Henry.

Peter paused.

Peter gasped.

Peter stared at the huge cardboard box. A time machine? *A time machine?* How could it be a time machine?

'It is not,' said Peter.

'Is too,' said Henry.

'But it's made of cardboard,' said Peter. 'And the washing machine came in it.'

Henry sighed.

'Don't you know anything? If it *looked* like a time machine everyone would try to steal it. It's a time machine in *disguise*.'

Peter looked at the time machine. On the one hand he didn't believe Henry for one minute. This was just one of Henry's tricks. Peter was a hundred million billion percent certain Henry was lying.

On the other hand, what if Henry *was* telling the truth for once and there was a real time machine in his sitting room?

'If it *is* a time machine I want to have a go,' said Peter.

'You can't. You're too young,' said Henry.

'Am not.'

'Are too.'

Perfect Peter stuck out his bottom lip.

25

'I don't believe you anyway.'

Horrid Henry was outraged.

'Okay, I'll prove it. I'll go to the future right now. Stand back. Don't move.'

Horrid Henry leapt into the box and closed the lid. The Time Machine began to shudder and shake.

Then everything was still for a very long time.

Perfect Peter didn't know what to do. What if Henry was gone – forever? What if he were stuck in the future?

I could have his room, thought Peter.

I could watch whatever I wanted on telly.
I could –

Suddenly the box tipped over and
Horrid Henry staggered out.

'Wh-wh- where am I?' he stuttered.
Then he collapsed on the floor.

Peter stared at Henry.

Henry stared wildly at Peter.

'I've been to the future!' gasped Henry,
panting. 'It was amazing. Wow. I met
my great-great-great-grandson. He still
lives in this house. And he looks just like
me.'

'So he's ugly,' muttered Peter.

'What – did – you – say?' hissed Henry.

'Nothing,' said Peter quickly. He didn't
know what to think. 'Is this a trick,
Henry?'

'Course it isn't,' said Henry. 'And just
for that I won't let you have a go.'

'I can if I want to,' said Peter.

'You keep away from my time machine,'

27

said Henry. 'One wrong move and you'll get blasted into the future.'

Perfect Peter walked a few steps towards the time machine. Then he paused.

'What's it like in the future?'

'Boys wear dresses,' said Horrid Henry. 'And lipstick. People talk Ugg language. *You'd* probably like it. Everyone just eats vegetables.'

'Really?'

'And kids have loads of homework.'

Perfect Peter loved homework.

'Ooohh.' This Peter *had* to see. Just in case Henry *was* telling the truth.

'I'm going to the future and you can't stop me,' said Peter.

'Go ahead,' said Henry. Then he snorted. 'You can't go looking like that!'

'Why not?' said Peter.

''Cause everyone will laugh at you.'

Perfect Peter hated people laughing at him.

'Why?'

'Because to them you'll look weird. Are you sure you really want to go to the future?'

'Yes,' said Peter.

'Are you sure you're sure?'

'YES,' said Peter.

'Then I'll get you ready,' said Henry solemnly.

'Thank you, Henry,' said Peter. Maybe he'd been wrong about Henry. Maybe going to the future had turned him into a nice brother.

Horrid Henry dashed out of the sitting room.

Perfect Peter felt a quiver of excitement. The future. What if Henry really was telling the truth?

Horrid Henry returned carrying a large wicker basket. He pulled out an old red dress of Mum's, some lipstick, and a black frothy drink.

'Here, put this on,' said Henry.

Perfect Peter put on the dress. It dragged onto the floor.

'Now, with a bit of lipstick,' said Horrid Henry, applying big blobs of red lipstick all over Peter's face, 'you'll fit right in. Perfect,' he said, standing back to admire his handiwork. 'You look just like a boy from the future.'

'Okay,' said Perfect Peter.

'Now listen carefully,' said Henry. 'When you arrive, you won't be able to speak the language unless you drink this bibble babble drink. Take this with you and drink it when you get there.'

Henry held out the frothy black drink from his Dungeon Drink Kit. Peter took it.

'You can now enter the time machine.' Peter obeyed. His heart was pounding.

'Don't get out until the time machine has stopped moving completely. Then count to twenty-five, and open the hatch very very slowly. You don't want a bit of you in the twenty-third century, and the rest here in the twenty-first. Good luck.'

Henry swirled the box round and round and round. Peter began to feel dizzy. The drink sloshed on the floor.

Then everything was still.

Peter's head was spinning. He counted to twenty-five, then crept out.

He was in the sitting room of a house that looked just like his. A boy wearing a bathrobe and silver waggly antennae with his face painted in blue stripes stood in front of him.

'Ugg?' said the strange boy.

'Henry?' said Peter.

'Uggg uggg bleuch ble bloop,' said the boy.

'Uggg uggg,' said Peter uncertainly.

'Uggh uggh drink ugggh,' said the boy, pointing to Peter's bibble babble drink.

Peter drank the few drops which were left.

'I'm Zog,' said Zog. 'Who are you?'

'I'm Peter,' said Peter.

'Ahhhhh! Welcome! You must be my great-great-great-uncle Peter. Your very nice brother Henry told me all about you when he visited me from the past.'

'Oh, what did he say?' said Peter.

'That you were an ugly toad.'

'I am not,' said Peter. 'Wait a minute,' he added suspiciously. 'Henry said that boys wore dresses in the future.'

'They do,' said Zog quickly. 'I'm a girl.'

'Oh,' said Peter. He gasped. Henry

would *never* in a million years say he was
a girl. Not even if he were being poked
with red hot pokers. Could it be. . .

Peter looked around. 'This looks just
like my sitting room.'

Zog snorted.

'Of course it does, Uncle Pete. This is
now the Peter Museum. You're famous in
the future. Everything has been kept
exactly as it was.'

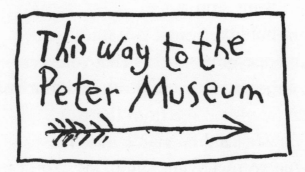

Peter beamed. He was famous in the
future. He always knew he'd be famous. A
Peter Museum! He couldn't wait to tell
Spotless Sam and Tidy Ted.

There was just one more thing . . .

'What about Henry?' he asked. 'Is he famous too?'

'Nah,' said Zog smoothly. 'He's known as What's-His-Name, Peter's older brother.'

Ahh. Peter swelled with pride. Henry was in his lowly place, at last. That proved it. He'd really travelled to the future!

Peter looked out the window. Strange how the future didn't look so different from his own time.

Zog pointed.

'Our spaceships,' he announced.

Peter stared. Spaceships looked just like cars.

'Why aren't they flying?' said Peter.

'Only at night time,' said Zog. 'You can either drive 'em or fly 'em.'

'Wow,' said Peter.

'Don't *you* have spaceships?' said Zog.

'No,' said Peter. 'Cars.'

'I didn't know they had cars in olden

days,' said Zog. 'Do you have blitzkatrons and zappersnappers?'

'No,' said Peter. 'What – '

The front door slammed. Mum walked in. She stared at Peter.

'What on earth. . .'

'Don't be scared,' said Peter. 'I'm Peter. I come from the past. I'm your great-great-great grandfather.'

Mum looked at Peter.

Peter looked at Mum.

'Why are you wearing my dress?' said Mum.

'It's not one of *yours*, silly,' said Peter.

'It belonged to my mum.'

'I see,' said Mum.

'Come on, Uncle Pete,' said Zog quickly, taking Peter firmly by the arm, 'I'll show you our supersonic hammock in the garden.'

'Okay, Zog,' said Peter happily.

Mum beamed.

'It's so lovely to see you playing nicely with your brother, Henry.'

Perfect Peter stood still.

'What did you call him?'

'Henry,' said Mum.

Peter felt a chill.

'So his name's not Zog? And he's not a girl?'

'Not the last time I looked,' said Mum.

'And this house isn't . . . the Peter Museum?'

Mum glared at Henry. 'Henry! Have you been teasing Peter again?'

'Ha ha tricked you!' shrieked Henry.

'Na Na Ne Nah Nah, wait till I tell everybody!'

'NO!' squealed Peter. 'NOOOOOOO!' How *could* he have believed his horrible brother?

'Henry! You horrid boy! Go to your room! No TV for the rest of the day,' said Mum.

But Horrid Henry didn't care. The Mega-Mean Time Machine would go down in history as his greatest trick ever.

3

PERFECT PETER'S REVENGE

Perfect Peter had had enough. Why oh
why did he always fall for Henry's tricks?

Every time it happened he swore Henry
would never ever trick him again. And
every time he fell for it. How *could* he
have believed that there were fairies at the
bottom of the garden? Or that there was
such a thing as a Fangmangler? But the
time machine was the worst. The very
very worst. Everyone had teased him.
Even Goody-Goody Gordon asked him
if he'd seen any spaceships recently.

Well, never again. His mean, horrible
brother had tricked him for the very last
time.

I'll get my revenge, thought Perfect Peter, pasting the last of his animal stamps into his album. I'll make Henry sorry for being so mean to me.

But what horrid mean nasty thing could he do? Peter had never tried to be revenged on anyone.

He asked Tidy Ted.

'Mess up his room,' said Ted.

But Henry's room was already a mess.

He asked Spotless Sam.

'Put a spaghetti stain on his shirt,' said Sam.

But Henry's shirts were already stained.

Peter picked up a copy of his favourite magazine *Best Boy*. Maybe it would have some handy hints on the perfect revenge. He searched the table of contents:

- IS YOUR BEDROOM AS TIDY AS IT COULD BE?
- TEN TOP TIPS FOR PLEASING YOUR PARENTS
- HOW TO POLISH YOUR TROPHIES

- WHY MAKING YOUR BED IS GOOD FOR YOU
- READERS TELL US ABOUT THEIR FAVOURITE CHORES!

Reluctantly, Peter closed *Best Boy* magazine. Somehow he didn't think he'd find the answer inside. He was on his own.

I'll tell Mum that Henry eats sweets in his bedroom, thought Peter. Then Henry would get into trouble. Big big trouble.

But Henry got into trouble all the time. That wouldn't be anything special.

I know, thought Peter, I'll hide Mr Kill. Henry would never admit it, but he couldn't sleep without Mr Kill. But so what if Henry couldn't sleep? He'd just come and jump on Peter's head or sneak downstairs and watch scary movies.

I have to think of something really, really horrid, thought Peter. It was hard for Peter to think horrid thoughts, but Peter was determined to try.

He would call Henry a horrid name, like Ugly Toad or Poo Poo face. *That* would show him.

But if I did Henry would hit me, thought Peter.

Wait, he could tell everyone at school that Henry wore nappies. Henry the big nappy. Henry the big smelly nappy. Henry nappy face. Henry poopy pants. Peter smiled happily. That would be a perfect revenge.

Then he stopped smiling. Sadly, no one at school would believe that Henry still wore nappies. Worse, they might think that Peter still did! Eeeek.

I've got it, thought Peter, I'll put a muddy twig in Henry's bed. Peter had

read a great story about a younger brother
who'd done just that to a mean older one.
That would serve Henry right.

But was a muddy twig enough revenge
for all of Henry's crimes against him?

No it was not.

I give up, thought Peter, sighing. It
was hopeless. He just couldn't think of
anything horrid enough.

Peter sat down on his beautifully made
bed and opened *Best Boy* magazine.

TELL MUM HOW MUCH YOU LOVE HER!

shrieked the headline.

And then a dreadful thought tiptoed

into his head. It was so dreadful, and so
horrid, that Perfect Peter could not
believe that he had thought it.

'No,' he gasped. 'I couldn't.' That was
too evil.

But . . . but . . . wasn't that exactly what
he wanted? A horrid revenge on a horrid
brother?

'Don't do it!' begged his angel.

'Do it!' urged his devil, thrilled to get
the chance to speak. 'Go on, Peter!

Henry deserves it.'

YES! thought Peter. He would do it.
He would be revenged!

Perfect Peter sat down at the computer.
Tap tap tap.

Dear Margaret,
I love you. Will you marry me?

Peter printed out the note and carefully
scrawled:

HENry

There! thought Peter proudly. That
looks just like Henry's writing. He folded
the note, then sneaked into the garden,
climbed over the wall, and left it on the

table inside Moody Margaret's Secret
Club tent.

'Of course Henry loves me,' said Moody
Margaret, preening. 'He can't help it.
Everyone loves me because I'm so lovable.'

'No you're not,' said Sour Susan. 'You're
moody. And you're mean.'
    'Am not!'

'Are too!'

'Am not. You're just jealous 'cause no one would *ever* want to marry you,' snapped Margaret.

'I am not jealous. Anyway, Henry likes *me* the best,' said Susan, waving a folded piece of paper.

'Says who?'

'Says Henry.'

Margaret snatched the paper from Susan's hand and read:

TO THE BEAUTIFUL SUSAN

Oh Susan,
No one is as pretty as you,
You always smell lovely
Just like shampoo.
HENRY

Margaret sniffed. 'Just like dog poo, you mean.'

'I do not,' shrieked Susan.

'Is this your idea of a joke?' snorted
Moody Margaret, crumpling the poem.

Sour Susan was outraged.

'No. It was waiting for me on the club-
house table. You're just jealous because
Henry didn't write *you* a poem.'

'Huh,' said Margaret. Well, she'd show
Henry. No one made a fool of her.

Margaret snatched up a pen and
scribbled a reply to Henry's note.

'Take this to Henry and report straight
back,' she ordered. 'I'll wait here for Linda
and Gurinder.'

'Take it yourself,' said Susan sourly. Why
oh why was she friends with such a
mean, moody jealous grump?

Horrid Henry was inside the Purple
Hand Fort plotting death to the Secret
Club and scoffing biscuits when an
enemy agent peered through the
entrance.

'Guard!' shrieked Henry.

But that miserable worm toad was
nowhere to be found.

Henry reminded himself to sack Peter
immediately.

'Halt! Who goes there?'

'I have an important message,' said the
Enemy.

'Make it snappy,' said Henry. 'I'm busy.'

Susan crept beneath the branches.

'Do you really like my shampoo,
Henry?' she asked.

Henry stared at Susan. She had a sick
smile on her face, as if her stomach hurt.

'Huh?' said Henry.

'You know, my *shampoo*,' said Susan, simpering.

Had Susan finally gone mad?

'*That's* your message?' said Horrid Henry.

'No,' said Susan, scowling. She tossed a scrunched-up piece of paper at Henry and marched off.

Henry opened the note:

I wouldn't marry you if you were the last creature on earth and that includes slimy toads and rattlesnakes. So there.

Margaret

Henry choked on his biscuit. Marry
Margaret?! He'd rather walk around town
carrying a Walkie-Talkie-Burpy-Slurpy-
Teasy-Weasy Doll. He'd rather learn
long division. He'd rather trade all his
computer games for a Princess Pamper
Parlour. He'd rather . . . he'd rather . . .
he'd rather marry Miss Battle-Axe than
marry Margaret!

What on earth had given Margaret the crazy, horrible, revolting idea he wanted to marry *her*?

He always knew Margaret was nuts. Now he had proof. Well well well, thought Horrid Henry gleefully. Wouldn't he tease her! Margaret would never live this down.

Henry leapt over the wall and burst into the Secret Club Tent.

'Margaret, you old pants face, I wouldn't marry you if –'

'Henry loves Margaret! Henry loves Margaret!' chanted Gorgeous Gurinder.

'Henry loves Margaret! Henry loves Margaret!' chanted Lazy Linda, making horrible kissing sounds.

Henry tried to speak. He opened his mouth. Then he closed it.

'No I don't,' gasped Horrid Henry.

'Oh yeah?' said Gurinder.

'Yeah,' said Henry.

'Then why'd you send her a note saying you did?'

'I didn't!' howled Henry.

'And you sent Susan a poem!' said Linda.

'I DID NOT!' howled Henry even louder. What on earth was going on? He took a step backwards.

The Secret Club members advanced on him, shrieking, 'Henry loves Margaret, Henry loves Margaret.'

Time, thought Horrid Henry, to beat a strategic retreat. He dashed back to his fort, the terrible words 'Henry loves Margaret' burning his ears.

'PETER!' bellowed Horrid Henry.
'Come here this minute!'

Perfect Peter crept out of the house to
the fort. Henry had found out about the
note and the poem. He was dead.

Goodbye, cruel world, thought Peter.

'Did you see anyone going into the
Secret Club carrying a note?' demanded
Henry, glaring.

Perfect Peter's heart began to beat
again.

'No,' said Peter. That wasn't a lie
because he hadn't seen himself.

'I want you to stand guard by the wall,
and report anyone suspicious to me at
once,' said Henry.

'Why?' said Peter innocently.

'None of your business, worm,' snapped
Henry. 'Just do as you're told.'

'Yes, Lord High Excellent Majesty of
the Purple Hand,' said Perfect Peter. What
a lucky escape!

Henry sat on his Purple Hand throne and considered. Who was this foul fiend? Who was this evil genius? Who was spreading these foul rumours? He had to find out, then strike back hard before the snake struck again.

But who'd want to be his enemy? He was such a nice, kind, friendly boy.

True, Rude Ralph wasn't very happy when Henry called him Ralphie Walfie.

Tough Toby wasn't too pleased when Henry debagged him during playtime.

And for some reason, Brainy Brian didn't see the joke when Henry scribbled all over his book report.

Vain Violet said she'd pay Henry back for pulling her pigtails.

And just the other day Fiery Fiona said Henry would be sorry he'd laughed during her speech in assembly.

Even Kind Kasim warned Henry to stop being so horrid or he'd teach him a lesson he wouldn't forget.

But maybe Margaret was behind the whole plot. He had stinkbombed her Secret Club, after all.

Hmmn. The list of suspects was rather long.

It had to be Ralph. Ralph loved playing practical jokes.

Well, it's not funny, Ralph, thought Horrid Henry. Let's see how *you* like it. Perhaps a little poem to Miss Battle-Axe . . .

Horrid Henry grabbed a piece of paper and began to scribble:

Oh Boudicca dear,
Whenever you're near,
I just want to cheer,
Oh big old teacher
Your carrot nose is your best feature
You are so sweet
I would like to kiss your feet
What a treat
Even though they smell of meat
Dear Miss Battle-Axe
Clear out your earwax
So you can hear me say...
No need to frown
But your pants are falling down!

Ha ha ha ha ha,
thought Henry.
He'd sign the
poem 'Ralph', get
to school early and
pin the poem on

the door of the Girls' Toilet. Ralph would
get into big big trouble.

But wait.

What if Ralph *wasn't* responsible?

Could it be Toby after all? Or Margaret?

There was only one thing to do. Henry
copied his poem seven times, signing each
copy with a different name. He would
post them all over school tomorrow. One
of them was sure to be guilty.

Henry sneaked into school, then quickly
pinned up his poems on every notice-
board. That done, he swaggered onto the
playground. Revenge is sweet, thought
Horrid Henry.

There was a crowd gathered outside the
boys' toilets.

'What's going on?' shrieked Horrid
Henry, pushing and shoving his way
through the crowd.

'Henry loves Margaret,' chanted Tough
Toby.

'Henry loves Margaret,' chanted Rude
Ralph.

Uh oh.

Henry glanced at the toilet door. There
was a note taped on it.

Dear Margaret,
I love you. Will you marry me?
HENry

Henry's blood froze. He ripped the note off the door.

'Margaret wrote it to herself,' blustered Horrid Henry.

'Didn't!' said Margaret.

'Did!' said Henry.

'Besides, you love *me!*' shrieked Susan.

'No I don't!' shrieked Henry.

'That's 'cause you love me!' said Margaret.

'I hate you!' shouted Henry.

'I hate you more!' said Margaret.

'I hate *you* more,' said Henry.

'You started it,' said Margaret.

'Didn't.'

'Did! You asked me to marry you.'

'NO WAY!' shrieked Henry.

'And you sent me a poem!' said Susan.

'No I didn't!' howled Henry.

'Well, if you didn't then who did?' said Margaret.

Silence.

'Henry,' came a little voice, 'can we play pirates after school today?'

Horrid Henry thought an incredible thought.

Moody Margaret thought an incredible thought.

Sour Susan thought an incredible thought.

Three pairs of eyes stared at Perfect Peter.

'Wha . . . what?' said Peter.

Uh oh.

'HELP!' shrieked Perfect Peter. He turned and ran.

'AAAARRRRGHHHHHH!' shrieked Horrid Henry, chasing after him. 'You're dead meat, worm!'

Miss Battle-Axe marched onto the playground. She was clutching a sheaf of papers in her hand.

'Margaret! Brian! Ralph! Toby! Violet! Kasim! Fiona! What is the meaning of these poems? Straight to the head – now!'

Perfect Peter crashed into her.

Smash!

Miss Battle-Axe toppled backwards into the bin.

'And you too, Peter,' gasped Miss Battle-Axe.

'Waaaaaaa!' wailed Perfect Peter. From now on, he'd definitely be sticking to good deeds. Whoever said revenge was sweet didn't have a horrid brother like Henry.

4

HORRID HENRY DINES AT RESTAURANT LE POSH

'Great news, everyone,' said Mum, beaming. 'Aunt Ruby is taking us all out for dinner to Le Posh, the best French restaurant in town.'

'Oh boy, Restaurant Le Posh,' said Perfect Peter. 'We've never been there.'

Horrid Henry stopped scribbling all over Peter's stamp album. His heart sank. French? Restaurant? Oh no. That meant strange, horrible, yucky food. That meant no burgers, no ketchup, no pizza. That meant –

'NOOOOOOOOOOO! I don't want to

go there!' howled Henry. Who knew what revolting poison would arrive on his plate, covered in gloopy sauce with green bits floating about. Uggghh.

'It's Mum's birthday,' said Dad, 'so we're celebrating.'

'I only like Whopper Whoopee,' said Henry. 'Or Fat Frank's. I don't want to go to Le Posh.'

'But Henry,' said Perfect Peter, tidying up his toys, 'it's a chance to try new food.'

Mum beamed. 'Quite right, Peter. It's always nice to try new things.'

'No it isn't,' snarled Horrid Henry. 'I hate trying new food when there's nothing wrong with the old.'

'I love it,' said Dad. 'I eat everything except tomatoes.'

'And I eat everything except squid,' said Mum.

'And I love all vegetables except beetroot,' said Perfect Peter. 'Especially spinach and sprouts.'

'Well I don't,' shrieked Horrid Henry. 'Do they have pasta?'

'Whatever they have will be delicious,' said Mum firmly.

'Do they have burgers? If they don't I'm not going,' wailed Horrid Henry.

Mum looked at Dad.

Dad looked at Mum.

Last time they'd taken Henry to a fancy restaurant he'd had a tantrum under the table. The time before he'd run screaming round the room snatching all the salt and pepper shakers and then thrown up on the people at the next table. The time

before that – Mum and Dad preferred
not to think about that.

'Shall we get a babysitter?' murmured
Dad.

'Leave him home on my birthday?'
murmured Mum. She allowed herself to be
tempted for a moment. Then she sighed.

'Henry, you are coming and you will be
on your best behaviour,' said Mum. 'Your
cousin Steve will be there. You wouldn't
want Steve to see you make a fuss, would
you?'

The hairs on the back of Henry's neck
stood up. Steve! Stuck-Up Steve! Horrid
Henry's arch-enemy and world's worst
cousin. If there was a slimier boy than
Steve slithering
around then
Horrid Henry
would eat
worms.

70

Last time they'd met Henry had tricked
Steve into thinking there was a monster
under his bed. Steve had sworn revenge.
There was nothing Steve wouldn't do to
get back at Henry.

Boy, did Horrid Henry hate Stuck-Up
Steve.

Boy, did Stuck-Up Steve hate Horrid
Henry.

'I'm not coming and that's final!'
screamed Horrid Henry.

'Henry,' said Dad. 'I'll make a deal with
you.'

'What deal?' said Henry. It was always
wise to be suspicious when parents
offered deals.

'I want you to be pleasant and talk to
everyone. And you will eat everything on
your plate like everyone else without
making a fuss. If you do, I'll give you £2.'

£2! Two whole pounds! Horrid Henry
gasped. Two whole pounds just for talking

and shoving a few
mouthfuls of
disgusting
food in his
mouth.

Normally he had to do that for free.

'How about £3?' said Henry.

'Henry . . .' said Mum.

'OK, deal,' said Horrid Henry. But I
won't eat a thing and they can't make me,
he thought. He'd find a way. Dad said he
had to eat everything on his plate. Well,
maybe some food wouldn't *stay* on his
plate. . . Horrid Henry smiled.

Perfect Peter stopped putting away his
bricks. He frowned. Shouldn't *he* get two
pounds like Henry?

'What's *my* reward for being good?' said
Perfect Peter.

'Goodness is its own reward,' said Dad.

★

The restaurant was hushed. The tables were covered in snowy-white tablecloths, with yellow silk chairs. Huge gold chandeliers dangled from the ceiling. Crystal glasses twinkled. The rectangular china plates sparkled. Horrid Henry was impressed.

'Wow,' said Henry. It was like walking into a palace.

'Haven't you ever been here before?' sneered Stuck-Up Steve.

'No,' said Henry.

'*We* eat here all the time,' said Steve. 'I guess you're too poor.'

'It's 'cause *we'd* rather eat at Whopper Whoopee,' lied Henry.

'Hush, Steve,' said Rich Aunt Ruby. 'I'm sure Whopper Whoopee is a lovely restaurant.'

Steve snorted.

Henry kicked him under the table.

'OWWWW!' yelped Steve. 'Henry kicked me!'

'No I didn't,' said Henry. 'It was an accident.'

'Henry,' said Mum through gritted teeth. 'Remember what we said about best behaviour? We're in a fancy restaurant.'

Horrid Henry scowled. He looked cautiously around. It was just as he'd feared. Everyone was busy eating weird

74

bits of this and that, covered in gloopy
sauces. Henry checked under the tables to
see if anyone was being sick yet.

There was no one lying poisoned under
the tables. I guess it's just a matter of time,
thought Henry grimly. You won't catch
me eating anything here.

Mum, Dad, Peter and Rich Aunt Ruby
blabbed away at their end of the table.
Horrid Henry sat sullenly next to Stuck-
Up Steve.

'I've got a new bike,' Steve bragged. 'Do you still have that old rust bucket you had last Christmas?'

'Hush, Steve,' said Rich Aunt Ruby.

Horrid Henry's foot got ready to kick Steve.

'Boudicca Battle-Axe! How many times have I told you – don't chew with your mouth open,' boomed a terrible voice.

Horrid Henry looked up. His jaw dropped.

There was his terrifying teacher, Miss Battle-Axe, sitting at a small table in the corner with her back to him. She was with someone even taller, skinnier, and

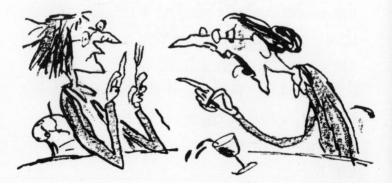

more ferocious than she was.

'And take your elbows off the table!'

'Yes, Mum,' said Miss Battle-Axe meekly.

Henry could not believe his ears. Did teachers have mothers? Did teachers ever leave the school? Impossible.

'Boudicca! Stop slouching!'

'Yes, Mum,' said Miss Battle-Axe, straightening up a fraction.

'So, what's everyone having?' beamed Aunt Ruby. Horrid Henry tore his eyes away from Miss Battle-Axe and stared at

the menu. It was entirely written in French.

'I recommend the mussels,' said Aunt Ruby.

'Mussels! Ick!' shrieked Henry.

'Or the blah blah blah blah blah.' Aunt Ruby pronounced a few mysterious French words.

'Maybe,' said Mum. She looked a little uncertain.

'Maybe,' said Dad. He looked a little uncertain.

'You order for me, Aunt Ruby,' said Perfect Peter. 'I eat everything.'

Horrid Henry had no idea what food Aunt Ruby had suggested, but he knew he hated every single thing on the menu.

'I want a burger,' said Henry.

'No burgers here,' said Mum firmly. 'This is Restaurant Le Posh.'

'I said I want a burger!' shouted Henry. Several diners looked up.

'Don't be horrid Henry!' hissed Mum.

'I CAN'T UNDERSTAND THIS MENU!' screamed Henry.

'Calm down this minute Henry,' hissed Dad. 'Or no £2.'

Mum translated: 'A tasty . . . uh . . . something on a bed of roast something with a something sauce.'

'Sounds delicious,' said Dad.

'Wait, there's more,' said Mum. 'A big piece of something enrobed with something cooked in something with carrots.'

'Right, I'm having that,' said Dad. 'I love carrots.'

Mum carried on translating. Henry opened his mouth to scream –

'Why don't you order *tripe*?' said Steve.

'What's that?' asked Henry suspiciously.

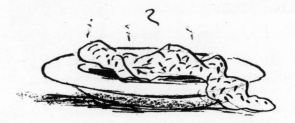

'You don't want to know,' said Steve.

'Try me,' said Henry.

'Intestines,' said Steve. 'You know, the wriggly bits in your stomach.'

Horrid Henry snorted. Sometimes he felt sorry for Steve. Did Steve really think he'd fool him with *that* old trick? *Tripe* was probably a fancy French word for spaghetti. Or trifle.

'Or you could order *escargots*,' said Steve. 'I dare you.'

'What's *escargots*?' said Henry.

Stuck-Up Steve stuck his nose in the air.

'Oh, sorry, I forgot you don't learn French at your school. *I've* been learning it for years.'

'Whoopee for you,' said Horrid Henry.

'*Escargots* are snails, stupid,' said Stuck-Up Steve.

Steve must think he was a real idiot, thought Horrid Henry indignantly. *Snails*. Ha ha ha. In a restaurant? As if.

'Oh yeah, right, you big fat liar,' said Henry.

Steve shrugged.

'Too chicken, huh?' he sneered. 'Cluck cluck cluck.'

Horrid Henry was outraged. No one called him chicken and lived.

'Course not,' said Horrid Henry. 'I'd love to eat snails.' Naturally it would turn out to be fish or something in a smelly, disgusting sauce, but so what? *Escargots* could hardly be more revolting than all the other yucky things on the menu. Steve would have to try harder than that to fool him. He would order so-called 'snails' just to show Steve up for the liar he was. Then wouldn't he make fun of stupid old Steve!

'And vat are ve having tonight?' asked
the French waiter.

Aunt Ruby ordered.

'An excellent choice, madame,' said the
waiter.

Dad ordered. The waiter kissed his
fingers.

'*Magnifique*, monsieur, our speciality.'

Mum ordered.

'Bravo, madame. And what about you,
young man?' the waiter asked Henry.

'I'm having *escargots,*' said Henry.

'Hmmn,' said the waiter. 'Monsieur is a
gourmet?'

Horrid Henry wasn't sure he liked the sound of that. Stuck-Up Steve snickered. What was going on? thought Horrid Henry.

'Boudicca! Eat your vegetables!'

'Yes, Mum.'

'Boudicca! Stop slurping.'

'Yes, Mum,' snapped Miss Battle-Axe.

'Boudicca! Don't pick your nose!'

'I wasn't!' said Miss Battle-Axe.

'Don't you contradict me,' said Mrs Battle-Axe.

The waiter reappeared, carrying six plates covered in silver domes.

'Voilà!' he said, whisking off the lids with a flourish. 'Bon appétit!'

Everyone peered at their elegant plates.

'Ah,' said Mum, looking at her squid.

'Ah,' said Dad, looking at his stuffed tomatoes.

'Ah,' said Peter, looking at his beetroot mousse.

Horrid Henry stared at his food. It looked like − it couldn't be − oh my God, it was . . . SNAILS! It really was snails! Squishy squashy squidgy slimy slithery slippery snails. Still in their shells. Drenched in butter, but unmistakably snails. Steve had tricked him.

Horrid Henry's hand reached out to hurl the snails at Steve.

Stuck-Up Steve giggled.

Horrid Henry stopped and gritted his teeth. No way was he giving Steve the satisfaction of seeing him get into big trouble. He'd ordered snails and he'd eat snails. And when he threw up, he'd make sure it was all over Steve.

Horrid Henry grabbed his fork and plunged. Then he closed his eyes and popped the snail in his mouth.

Horrid Henry chewed.

Horrid Henry chewed some more.

'Hmmn,' said Horrid Henry.

He popped another snail in his mouth. And another.

'Yummy,' said Henry. 'This is brilliant.'
Why hadn't anyone told him that Le Posh
served such thrillingly revolting food?
Wait till he told Rude Ralph!

Stuck-Up Steve looked unhappy.

'How's your maggot sauce, Steve?' said
Henry cheerfully.

'It's not maggot sauce,' said Steve.

'Maggot maggot maggot,' whispered
Henry. 'Watch them wriggle about.'

Steve put down his fork. So did Mum,
Dad, and Peter.

'Go on everyone, eat up,' said Henry,
chomping.

'I'm not that hungry,' said Mum.

'You said we had to eat everything on
our plate,' said Henry.

'No I didn't,' said Dad weakly.

'You did too!' said Henry. 'So eat!'

'I don't like beetroot,' moaned Perfect
Peter.

'Hush, Peter,' snapped Mum.

86

'Peter, I never thought *you* were a fussy eater,' said Aunt Ruby.

'I'm not!' wailed Perfect Peter.

'Boudicca!' blasted Mrs Battle-Axe's shrill voice. 'Pay attention when I'm speaking to you!'

'Yes, Mum,' said Miss Battle-Axe.

'Why can't you be as good as that boy?' said Mrs Battle-Axe, pointing to Horrid Henry. 'Look at him sitting there, eating so beautifully.'

Miss Battle-Axe turned round and saw Henry. Her face went bright red, then

purple, then white. She gave him a sickly smile.

Horrid Henry gave her a little polite wave. Oh boy.

For the first time in his life was he ever looking forward to school.

HORRID HENRY

is also available on audio cassette and CD,
all read by Miranda Richardson

'A hoot from beginning to end ... As always,
Miranda Richardson's delivery is perfection and
the manic music is a delight.' *Daily Express*

'Long may this dreadful boy continue to
terrorise all who know him. He's a nightmare,
but so entertaining ... Miranda Richardson's
spirited reading is accompanied by a brilliant
music soundtrack – they make a noisy and
fun-filled duo.' *Parents' Guide*